Written and illustrated
by
David Bullock

PC
BEN

PC Ben went out for a walk on a bright and sunny morning.

He wore a jacket that was yellow.

On his head he had a hat.

He had a radio, handcuffs, a phone and a snack...

...and he walked around his beautiful town on that bright and sunny morning.

He met two men who didn't have a home.

He met their dog and gave it a bone.

He got them some blankets, some soup and some rolls.

Then he said farewell and carried on his patrols.

He went to a church.

He went to a shop.

He went right to the top of a parking lot
and from there he watched over his beautiful town on
that bright and sunny morning.

But as Ben looked down at the street below he saw
a lost old man who didn't know where to go.

Ben helped the man and got him back to his house.

Back to his wife and his garden...

...and a very fat mouse that was called Mrs WHIFF
and Ben soon found out why.

After lunch Ben continued to walk.

He walked and talked and talked and...

...TALKED to every single person that he met.

The doctor, the vicar, the postman, the vet.

He saw a pony, a pigeon, a snail and a swan.

And even when it rained
Ben still carried on, walking
and talking and keeping
people safe.

Then it got busy! A bus had broken down.

So PC Ben ran through the town.

To stop the traffic until the bus moved on.

The passengers were happy. They even sang a song.

A lady called the police and said 'I've lost my bike. It is big. It is green. It has dots and a stripe.'

Ben searched for that bike all around.

He checked up
a tree.

He looked underground.

Then he found it wedged behind an old park bench. It was stuck in the mud but with a bit of a wrench Ben pulled it free and got it straight back...

...to its owner whose name was Mrs BATT.

As it came close to Ben going home he heard a very loud ringing on his mobile phone.

He answered it, right there and then. He said 'Hello! Good afternoon, it's PC Ben.'

It was a shopkeeper about a thief who had taken some sweets. Who hadn't paid for the sweets and was eating the sweets.

Ben ran and found the
man and said 'It's wrong
to steal.' And in no time
he had struck a deal.

For the man to pay for the sweets he had pinched. To say sorry to the shopkeeper whose name was Mr Finch and to promise never to take another sweet again.

The shopkeeper was happy and so was Ben.

And then it came to the end of the day. Time for home, but on his way Ben said goodbye to those he had met.

The postman, the pony, the pigeon, the vet

He walked by the river...

...the castle...

...and the school.

But for PC Ben the best part of it all is not the end of the day, No, not at all, but tomorrow and the day after and the day after that. When he puts on his coat and he puts on his hat.

Because it's then when Ben can do it all again.

Printed in Great Britain
by Amazon